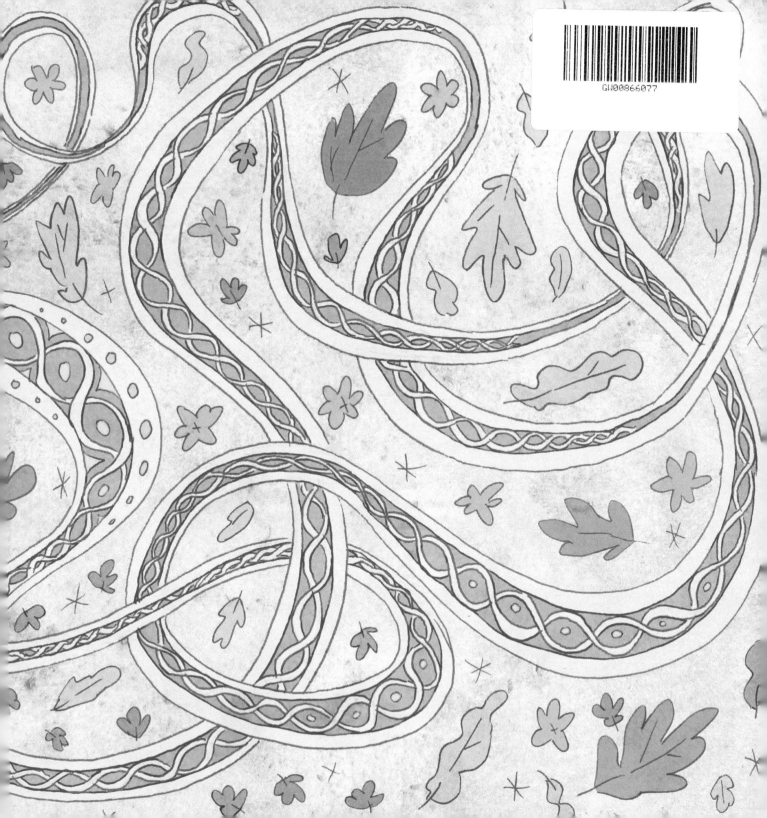

AuthorHouse™ UK
1663 Liberty Drive
Bloomington, IN 47403 USA
www.authorhouse.co.uk
UK TFN: 0800 0148641 (Toll Free inside the UK)
UK Local: 02036 956322 (+44 20 3695 6322 from outside the UK)

Illustrations by John Corrigan

This book is printed on acid-free paper.

ISBN: 978-1-6655-8052-6 (sc)
ISBN: 978-1-6655-8051-9 (e)

Print information available on the last page.

Published by AuthorHouse 12/21/2020

author HOUSE®

GUDRUN
AND THE MONSTERS IN THE WOOD

BRIGID CORRIGAN   JOHN CORRIGAN

Gudrun loved to discover how things work.

Her parents, it seemed, did not always share her curiosity.

Young Gudrun lived with her family in a
small town on the edge of a forest.
Nothing much ever happened there,
but that was about to change…

Mrs. Olsen *was* the first to see them

(although the sun was in her eyes)

Next it was Mr. Peterson's turn.

Late one evening, he heard their terrible screeches.

"By Thor, I've never heard their like" he whispered.

Thor – Viking god of thunder.

The Larsson twins also claimed to have encountered the monsters, (but they failed to mention why they were in the woods at night) The villagers became frightened and remained indoors after nightfall.

One evening Gudrun's father did not return at his usual hour.

Her mother left her in charge of Harald until she returned.

Gudrun promised she would look after her brother
and for a while she was as good as her word . . for a while.

But as soon as his sister was sleeping, Harald seized his chance and bolted through the unbolted door. Gudrun woke up in time to see him swallowed by the forest.

She edged her way to the edge of the wood.

Frightful screams made her blood run cold. . .

Whew, Only Mr. Nordstrom, scaring the
neighbours on his nightly naked walk.
She pressed on into the dense forest until
she came upon a cave.

Whoosh, her brother flew over her head!
An owl had mistaken him for a giant rat.
Realising his mistake he released him and Harald bounced
straight into the mouth of the cavern. She had to admire the
owl's accuracy. "That was a 3 pointer", she thought.

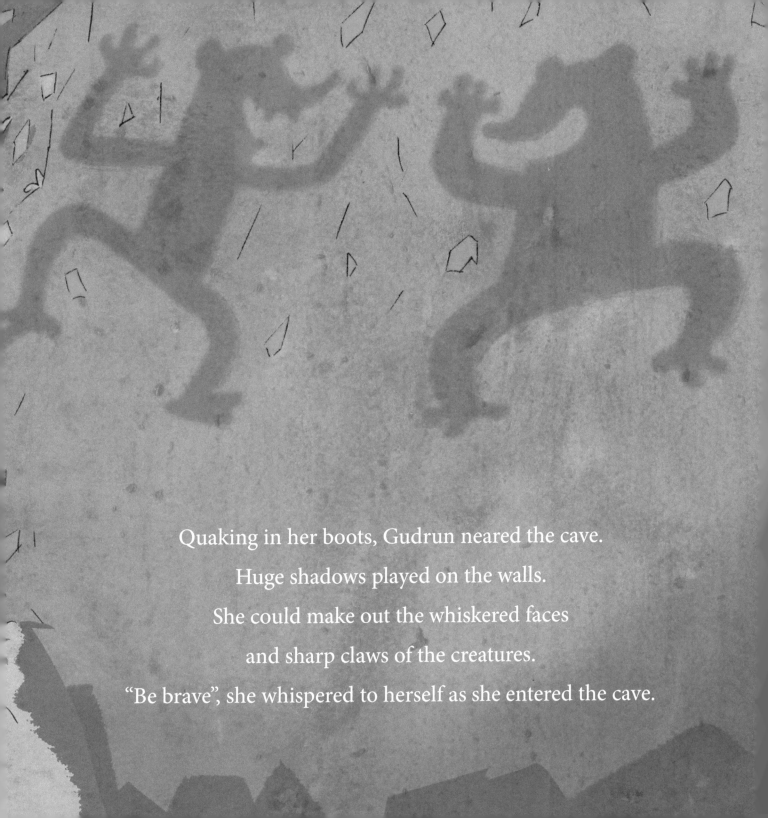

Quaking in her boots, Gudrun neared the cave.

Huge shadows played on the walls.

She could make out the whiskered faces

and sharp claws of the creatures.

"Be brave", she whispered to herself as she entered the cave.

But she was greeted not by monsters . . . but mice??
The cave had made shrieks from squeaks and the sun
had lengthened the shadows of the little critters.
She grabbed her brother's hand along with
2 of the mice and made for home.

Along the way they met their parents. Acrobatics always calmed them down (they had met during their time in the circus). Altogether they returned to their little house.

In the warmth of the kitchen Gudrun told of her adventure.

Her parents marvelled at her bravery.

Gudrun glowed.

Her story spread quickly and the townspeople felt a little flippin' stupid.

Imagine being afraid of mice!

But they did make good pets. Gudrun even managed to teach them some card tricks... although she never beat them at Viking holdup.

Thingmote

Mr Norstoms rock hut

Mrs Olafson's chalet

The Larsson twins' forge

Mrs Olsen's cottage

Old Mr. Peterson's hut

Lightning Source UK Ltd.
Milton Keynes UK
UKHW051052291220
375879UK00002B/25